Finley's
Perfect Pet

by Damian Harvey and Kathryn Selbert

FRANKLIN WATTS
LONDON·SYDNEY

Dad was reading the newspaper.

"Look," he said, "a new pet shop has opened up in town."

Finley looked at the picture of the pet shop.

"Can I have a pet?" he asked.

Mum and Dad said, "No."

"Why not?" asked Finley.

Mum told him that pets need lots of looking after.

"They can be hard work," agreed Dad.

"I would look after it," said Finley. "I promise."

"What do you think?" asked Mum.

"I suppose we could go and have a look
in Eli's Pet Shop," said Dad, smiling.

"Yes!" cried Finley.

The next day they all went to the pet shop.

While Dad talked to Eli at the counter,

Finley went to have a look round the shop.

"How about a goldfish?" said Mum.

"Fish seem a bit boring," said Finley.

"I'd like something more fun."

Eli pointed at a small hutch in the corner.

"A rabbit would be fun," she said.

But Finley had seen the perfect pet.

"No, thank you," he said. "I'd like
one of those."

"You're **not** having a parrot," said Dad.

"You can have a rabbit."

"But I **love** parrots," said Finley.

Mum and Dad looked at the parrots.

Then they looked at each other.

"All right, then," said Mum. "We'll give it

a try."

Finley, Mum and Dad put
the parrot's cage in the living room.
The parrot talked and squawked all night.
It kept everyone awake.
"Sorry, Finley. It'll have to go," said Mum.
Finley agreed.

The next morning, they took
the noisy parrot back to the pet shop.
Mum and Dad asked Eli for help again.
"A rabbit would be a good pet," said Eli.
"But I don't want a rabbit, thank you,"
said Finley.
Finley had already spotted something
that he wanted. It was lying
in a glass tank.

"You're **not** having a snake," cried Dad.

"You can have a rabbit."

"But I **love** snakes," said Finley.

Mum and Dad asked Eli if a snake was really a good pet for a family.

"Oh yes," said Eli. "This kind of snake could be perfect."

"All right," said Mum. "We'll give it a try."

At home, they put the snake
in a big tank.
"I hope he likes his new home,"
said Finley.
"I'm sure he will," said Mum.

Finley sat and watched his new pet.
He wondered what it would do.

The snake did not do anything. It just sat
and watched Finley. Then it fell asleep.
"This isn't much fun," said Finley.

11

The next morning the tank was empty.

There was no sign of the snake anywhere.

"He's escaped!" cried Finley.

"We'll find him," said Mum. "He can't

have gone far."

Dad searched in the kitchen. He looked under the sink and in all the cupboards. Mum looked in the bedrooms. She rooted in the cupboards and peered under the beds. Finley looked behind the chairs and under the table in the dining room. They could not find the snake.

"He could be anywhere," said Dad.

A week later, Dad was putting
some clothes away, when suddenly ...
"Snake!" he yelled.

There was Finley's snake, curled up and fast asleep in the cupboard.

"It's no good," said Dad. "We can't keep the snake. He'll have to go back."

Finley agreed.

In the morning, they took the sleepy snake

back to Eli's Pet Shop.

This time, Finley went to look at

the rabbits.

He watched them hop and jump.

Finley held one of the white rabbits
in his arms and gave it a stroke.
The rabbit twitched its nose.
"Can I have a rabbit, please?"
asked Finley.
Mum and Dad looked at each other and
smiled. "Yes," they replied. "We think that
a rabbit would be perfect."

Finley helped Mum build a cosy house for the rabbit.

The rabbit slept in its house all night.

In the daytime, the rabbit ran round the garden.

It dug holes in the lawn.

It ate lots of plants and flowers.

"I love my rabbit," said Finley.

"He's perfect."

Story order

Look at these 5 pictures and captions.
Put the pictures in the right order
to retell the story.

1

Finley chooses a parrot.

2

Finley chooses a rabbit.

3

The snake is missing.

4

There's a new pet shop in town.

5

The rabbit is perfect.

Independent Reading

This series is designed to provide an opportunity for your child to read on their own. These notes are written for you to help your child choose a book and to read it independently.

In school, your child's teacher will often be using reading books which have been banded to support the process of learning to read. Use the book band colour your child is reading in school to help you make a good choice. *Finley's Perfect Pet* is a good choice for children reading at Purple Band in their classroom to read independently.

The aim of independent reading is to read this book with ease, so that your child enjoys the story and relates it to their own experiences.

About the book

Finley and his parents head to the new pet shop in town to choose a pet for Finley. After Finley's first two pet choices cause a few problems for him at home, he decides a rabbit would be just right.

Before reading

Help your child to learn how to make good choices by asking: "Why did you choose this book? Why do you think you will enjoy it?" Look at the cover together and ask: "What do you think the story will be about?" Ask your child to think of what they already know about the story context. Then ask your child to read the title aloud. Ask: "Which pet do you think Finley will choose? Which would you choose: a snake, a rabbit or a parrot?"

Remind your child that they can sound out the letters to make a word if they get stuck.

Decide together whether your child will read the story independently or read it aloud to you.

During reading

Remind your child of what they know and what they can do independently. If reading aloud, support your child if they hesitate or ask for help by telling the word. If reading to themselves, remind your child that they can come and ask for your help if stuck.

After reading

Support comprehension by asking your child to tell you about the story. Use the story order puzzle to encourage your child to retell the story in the right sequence, in their own words. The correct sequence can be found on the next page.

Help your child think about the messages in the book that go beyond the story and ask: "Can there be a perfect pet for someone? Why or why not?"

Give your child a chance to respond to the story: "What was your favourite part? Why do you think Finley wanted a parrot at first?"

Extending learning

Help your child think more about the inferences in the story by asking: "What do you think Finley's parents think of the rabbit in the end? Why do you think that?"

In the classroom, your child's teacher may be teaching how to use speech marks when characters are speaking. There are many examples in this book that you could look at with your child. Find these together and point out how the end punctuation (comma, full stop, question mark or exclamation mark) comes inside the speech marks. Ask your child to read some examples out loud, adding appropriate expression.